This is My Book

Name _____

Date _____

This book was published
originally by Deere & Company in 1958. It
was distributed to farm families throughout
North America by John Deere farm equip-
ment dealerships. Since that time, Deere
has received literally hundreds of letters
requesting copies. It seems that those who
read the book as a child now want to share it
with their children or grandchildren. It is to
this new generation that this edition is
dedicated.

Copyright Deere & Company, 1988 • Moline, Illinois

Reprinted by the RC2 BRANDS,INC.
with permission of Deere & Company.

2004

ISBN 1-887327-15-0

JOHNNY TRACTOR
AND HIS PALS

A JOHN DEERE STORYBOOK FOR LITTLE FOLKS

From a Story by Louise Price Bell

Illustrated by Roy A. Bostrom, Retired Staff Artist, John Deere

The moon and stars were bright. It was night on the Fowler Farm. The lights in Farmer Fowler's house shone cheerfully.

The barnyard and fields were quiet. All the cows and pigs and chickens were fast asleep.

But behind the barn, Farmer Fowler's farm machines were wide awake. They were talking in very low voices. They have a special language of their own, just as trees and flowers do.

Johnny Tractor stood in the middle. He was their leader because he was a tractor. He was sure he was the most important machine on the farm.

And he knew he looked handsome in his shiny green and yellow coat and big black rubber tires.

Perry Plow was hitched behind Johnny Tractor. Early in the morning Farmer Fowler would come for them. Tomorrow would be the day to plow the field along the creek.

"Farmer Fowler wants a big wheat crop from that field this year," said Perry.

Dicky Disk growled. He had a deep voice. "That field is very dry, Perry," he said. "Farmer Fowler will use you to plow it. But then he will use me to cut up the clods of dirt."

Johnny Tractor scolded Dicky Disk. "Stop acting so proud," said Johnny. "Farmer Fowler also uses Henry Harrow to make the fields smooth."

This pleased Henry Harrow. He liked to get special attention from Johnny Tractor.

Then Henry Harrow spoke. His voice was soft and gentle like his gentle work in the fields.
"Well, sometimes Mr. Fowler does use me, too," Henry said as he flipped a speck of dirt off one of his many spikes. "I am always ready to do my part."

"I'm always ready to do my part, too," spoke up Danny Drill. "I plant the seeds for Farmer Fowler. I plant them just right so they will grow quickly and evenly. And I put fertilizer in the soil so the plants will have plenty of food.

"Sometimes," Danny Drill teased, "I think I'm as important as Johnny Tractor."

Before Johnny could say a word, Chucky Cultivator muttered: "I'm important, too. I get rid of the bad weeds that would keep the crops from growing. Why, if it weren't for me, Farmer Fowler's fields would be full of weeds instead of corn, beans, and potatoes."

All of the machines nodded and agreed, "Yes, Chucky, you're very valuable."

Johnny Tractor couldn't keep still another minute. He turned around so fast he made Perry Plow dizzy.

"Ha! What would you do without me, Chucky?
I pull you over the fields, you know," boasted Johnny,
spinning his steering wheel.

Johnny Tractor stuck out his chest and strutted around the group. "The truth is, I have to help all of you," he shouted. "I pull Micky Mower and Bobby Baler through the hay fields. And my big muscles turn Gary Grinder to make feed for the pigs, cows, and chickens. I'm the most important of all," Johnny roared proudly.

"Shhh," scolded big Clancy Combine, looking down his long green nose at Johnny. "You'll wake up the rooster. And besides, you're not so important. I don't need you at all. I do my work all by myself. I have my own engine. So there!"

Johnny Tractor couldn't think of any answer. So he yawned and pretended he was going to sleep. He knew Clancy Combine really didn't need him.

Johnny began to feel very ashamed of the way he'd acted. He said, "Well, I guess Farmer Fowler couldn't get along without any of us. He really needs all of us in some way."

All of the other machines agreed with Johnny Tractor.

"You better get some rest now if you're going to keep up with me tomorrow," Johnny added in a kind voice as he settled his wheels firmly on the ground and sighed.

Before long, the sun would chase the moon from the sky and the rooster would wake them all up with his "Cock-a-doodle-doo."

Tonight they must rest just as Farmer Fowler and his family were doing. Tomorrow they must be ready to work hard together.

Soon they were all fast asleep.